BARNEY
THE DUBLIN FOX

F.JOHN MCLAUGHLIN
ILLUSTRATED BY GORDON D'ARCY

AuthorHouse™
1663 Liberty Drive
Bloomington, IN 47403
www.authorhouse.com
Phone: 1 (833) 262-8899

This book is printed on acid-free paper.

ISBN: 978-1-7283-7102-3 (sc)
ISBN: 978-1-7283-7103-0 (hc)
ISBN: 978-1-7283-7101-6 (e)

Library of Congress Control Number: 2020916024

Print information available on the last page.

Published by AuthorHouse 08/31/2020

authorHOUSE®

CONTENTS

To My Grandson
John Bury Weld McLaughlin

Acknowledgments: Rosemarie Boyd; Anne Jackson, "Words are My Work"; Elizabeth McLaughlin and John Ganem for their help in bringing this tale to life.

Barney's map of Dublin

CHAPTER ONE

Rathcoffey Castle

Barney the fox awoke bright eyed and bushy tailed. It was springtime in Ireland. He had come to a painful decision. He was going to have to abandon his comfortable den in the county. His home was in the dungeons of Rathcoffey castle, in County Kildare. The castle was once an important part of the Pale, a semi-circular ring of castles built to protect the English in Dublin. The Pale protected their families, property, and cattle from the incursions of the wild Irish raiders. Hence, the expression, "Beyond the Pale", implied that if you were outside the Pale, you were on your own, unprotected. The castles were connected by six foot high ramparts with a deep ditch on either side. The tops of the rampart were flat. Thus, if a castle was attacked, rescuers could race out over the ramparts to their defense from the two castles on either side.

The ditches and ramparts prevented the English livestock from being rustled. The castle had lain in ruins for over three hundred years. It had been besieged and destroyed by cannon by General Monk in 1642. The owners of the castle had mistakenly supported the losing side in the English civil war. Oliver Cromwell's forces had prevailed.

The castle's dungeons had provided a magnificent den for generations of foxes. Alas, two recent unrelated developments, totally beyond Barney's control, were making the foxes lives unbearable. First of all, in 2009, the English parliament had outlawed fox hunting. Bravo, thought Barney when he first heard the news at the monthly midnight foxes meeting on the Curragh. Not one of the foxes foresaw the consequences of this decision. It was alright for those superior aristocratic English foxes to stroll around the countryside without fear of persecution. Now the infuriated hunters of England were swarming into Ireland, as if they owned the country, to aggressively hunt foxes. The peaceful Kildare Hunt with their lazy pack of hunts, used to trot out once or twice a month to halfheartedly chase a few slow old foxes for a bit of crack and after an hour retire to Straffan House Hotel for happy hour and to be photographed by the visiting American tourists.

Now the Kildare Hunt was out in full cry three days a week from dawn to dusk. The pack of foxhounds had doubled in size, augmented by aggressive

Barney and family in their den with foxhounds furiously trying to reach them

redundant English hounds. Foxes were being caught with increasing frequency and ripped to pieces by the pack. It was all a bit much.

Barney's five cubs had been hunted twice while playing outside their den. They had barely escaped into the den with their lives. Barney had retrieved two cannonballs from General Monk's siege. They were able to wedge the balls, in the nick of time, into the den's front and back entrances, thus preventing the infuriated hounds from entering. His wife, Molly, a vixen, was in hysterics. His five cubs were shivering in the corner of the den, terrified.

The second unforeseen disaster was the invention of metal detectors, first invented for the military to locate unexploded bombs and mines in times of war. Now they were on sale to the general public. Hordes of teenagers appeared with metal detectors to hunt for discarded weapons, swords, guns, and cannon balls in the ruins of the castle. Armed with shovels they were incessantly digging holes to find buried treasure. It would only be a matter of time before they dug through the castle ruins, attracted by the loud signal from the cannonballs, and break into their den. It was definitely time for Barney to scout for a new home. Staying in the country was not an option.

All the Irish hunts across the country had been invigorated by the influx of English hunters and hounds. It was time for Barney to move his family into the safety of Dublin city, twenty-five miles away. Before he left to search for a home he decided to move his family into the adjacent Rathcoffey Mansion. The three story building was roofless and windowless. The open doorways were barricaded, in true Irish fashion, with old metal bed frames, high enough to prevent hunters and fox hounds from entering the ruins. The current residents were a band of vicious feral cats.

Barney cautiously approached Rufus the leader of the cats, who was basking in the sunshine on a broad window ledge. He proposed to Rufus that he would like to rent the kitchen in the basement as a temporary residence for his family. Rufus, recognizing opportunity when it came knocking, said that he would happily rent out the kitchen for ten mice a month and asked craftily for a deposit of ten mice to cover damages before the foxes were allowed on the property. Barney, realizing that he had no choice, promptly accepted the exorbitant rent. He hoped it would only be for a short period of time. His next challenge was to find twenty mice. Where could he find so many mice? He sat and pondered in deep thought. Suddenly, the answer came to him like a lightning bolt.

The previous year he had taken his eldest cub, Sean, on a nocturnal hunting expedition. When they were passing through the neighboring town of Clane, they had been astonished to see mice running amuck in the Clane Bakery and Café. That night, Barney barricaded his family into the castle den and then set out on a reconnaissance mission. He was delighted to see fifty mice scurrying around the bakery and café. He quietly retreated. The following night he returned with his entire family. The previous night he had noted that the owners of the café left the basement windows ajar for ventilation. He was able to slip his paw in, release the catch, and open the window. Silently the foxes trooped in. Barney had Joyce, the lightest and most agile of his cubs, jump into a large sack of white flour. She emerged like a ghost. He then instructed her to silently enter the dining room and leap onto the white table in the middle of the room and then to lie prone. The busy mice failed to notice Joyce's ghostly arrival. They were intent on finding every last crumb. Barney then dispatched his four boys to slowly crawl into the room following the walls until they each came to a mouse hole.

Barney and Molly hid by the entrances to the dining room and the kitchen. They all lay prone, barely breathing, until the bells of St. Michael and all Angels rang out at midnight. Joyce, on hearing the bells, stood up and barked. The mice panicked. They raced towards the doorways and their mouse holes. The foxes pounced and pounced. Within five minutes, thirty mice lay dead on the floor.

Barney ran into the kitchen and borrowed a cake tin. They filled the tin with dead mice and retreated to their dungeon den. They celebrated their successful raid by consuming ten mice. They surprised Rufus, the cat, with their tin full of mice. With their deposit and rent paid in full, they moved into their new home the following night.

There was only one entrance into the mansion basement, an old scullery paneless window, large enough for a fox or cat to enter but far too small for a foxhound. Molly, the vixen was in charge of moving their provisions from the dungeon into the larder of the old kitchen. She organized her cubs into a team. Red removed the fruit and vegetables stored in the dungeon and brought them to the entrance. Seamus and Liam flew backwards and forwards across the moonlit yard to the scullery window, and then they dropped their previous cargo into the basement. Joyce, who had the best organization skills, was in charge of stacking their provisions safely in the larder. Barney stood guard with Sean on the lookout for any nocturnal foxhounds. The whole operation went like clockwork.

Hunting mice in the Clane coffee house

There was only one entrance into the mansion basement, an old scullery paneless window, large enough for a fox or cat to enter but far too small for a foxhound. Molly, the vixen was in charge of moving their provisions from the dungeon into the larder of the old kitchen. She organized her cubs into a team. Red removed the fruit and vegetables stored in the dungeon and brought them to the entrance. Seamus and Liam flew backwards and forwards across the moonlit yard to the scullery window, and then they dropped their previous cargo into the basement. Joyce, who had the best organization skills, was in charge of stacking their provisions safely in the larder. Barney stood guard with Sean on the lookout for any nocturnal foxhounds. The whole operation went like clockwork.

Molly and her cubs felt secure in their new home. They knew that any foxhound attempting to break into the mansion would be greeted by thirty ferocious feral cats. Barney, content that his family was safe, prepared for his departure. He borrowed a scarf from farmer John's scarecrow and packed his provisions for the trip. He put apples, nuts, plums, and carrots into the scarf, tied the four corners, and wrapped the scarf around a stout stick.

Barney left at dusk with the stick and his provisions over his shoulder. He had to travel ten miles across country. He gave the towns of Clane and Naas a

Barney escapes on the Guiness lorry while foxhounds dig
in the yard and beer-drinkers enjoy the drama

wide berth, arriving in the town of Kilcullen at dawn. Tired and exhausted, he crept into the yard of the Hideout Bar and Grill, slipped into the barn and scaled five bales of hay. It was a Monday morning. He breakfasted on his provisions from his sack and then fell sound asleep. Suddenly, he was awoken by the clash of empty barrels being thrown into the back of a Guinness truck. Barney had known that on a Monday afternoon the truck would arrive to pick up the empty barrels from the weekend. It was his transport to Dublin. He waited until the last barrel was loaded. Then he leaped up onto the bed of the truck and wedged himself behind two barrels. The driver then swung the tailgate shut and secured the latches. Suddenly, the yard exploded into chaos.

The Kildare foxhounds flew into the yard. They had picked up his scent. They raced into the barn and started ripping hay bales apart. Then the hunters arrived, desperately trying to get the hounds under control. All the locals, beer in hand, streamed out of the bar to watch the excitement. Barney couldn't help himself. He raised his paw and waved farewell to the hounds. The foxhounds, seeing their quarry disappearing, frantically raced after the accelerating truck. The town of Kilcullen hadn't seen so much excitement since the racehorse, Arkle, won the Irish Grand National in 1964.

CHAPTER TWO

Dublin

Barney spent the entire trip to Dublin fending off wayward barrels as they bounced around the back of the truck. Battered and bruised, he was greatly relieved when the truck finally turned off James's Street, through the dark blue gates into Guinness's brewery.

As it was after six o'clock, the driver and his mate left the truck in the yard for unloading in the morning. They proceeded to the bar in the yard for their complimentary pint of Guinness before proceeding home. When all was quiet, Barney stiffly hopped down from the truck. He entered the first open doorway and found a plump rat fast asleep on the floor. Barney said to himself, "Perfect, dinner is served." He then retired to the back of the shed and fell asleep on a pile of old tarpaulins. He was delighted with himself, he was in Dublin.

He awoke to find himself surrounded by five feral alley cats. He yawned and bared his sharp teeth. With startled meows the cats fled in all directions. They did not fear dogs however; they realized that a fox was a completely different kettle of fish.

The brewery gates opened at six o'clock in the morning. Barney slipped out into the street. He was terrified by the roar of the early morning traffic. As dawn approached he realized that he had to go to ground as soon as possible. He raced along the pavement towards the city. The first open ground he came to was Christ Church Cathedral.

He delved into the thick shrubbery around the Cathedral. He surprised two badgers enjoying the fresh morning air. They were stunned by the sudden appearance of a wild fox in their refuge. Barney gruffly apologized for disturbing their peace. He explained that he had just arrived from the country on a mission to find a new home in the city. Once the badgers realized that Barney had no intention of attacking them or chasing them through the streets, they relaxed and introduced themselves.

They were two brothers, Brian and Paddy, about to embark on a walking tour of the Wicklow Mountains, to the south of Dublin, in search of the elusive wild spring mushrooms, their favorite delicacy. They invited Barney to join them for breakfast in their sett (home) beneath the shrubbery. It was time to go underground as the archbishop's Springer Spaniels were usually released from the residence about that time. They loved to chase any animal with a tail. The badgers led Barney into the thickest part of the shrubbery, and then promptly disappeared.

Barney was puzzled, where had his new hosts gone? He took three steps forward then fell three feet into a hole in the ground. He landed on a smooth earthen floor. He was in a spacious room with a small turf fire in the corner. Two hedgehogs were fast asleep in front of the fire. The smoke disappeared through an old rabbit hole in the ceiling. He discovered that a badger's home, called a sett, was much larger and more elaborate than a fox's den. The ceiling was high enough to allow the badgers and the fox to stand upright. The walls were decorated with artifacts from the original Viking settlements, a thousand years earlier.

Brian and Paddy had decorated the walls of their living room with broad swords, golden brooches, and necklaces they had found excavating in the cathedral grounds. One entire wall was painted with a scene of Viking ships arriving in Dublin Bay, with Howth Head in the background. The mural had been painted by Peadair, an itinerant goose artist over a hundred years earlier.

The badgers had a long low table set up for breakfast. Brian unobtrusively laid an extra place for Barney. They explained that they liked to dine, Roman

Barney invited to dine with badgers in their living room

style, lying beside the table and helping themselves from the smorgasbord. Barney was There were tomatoes, beets, potatoes, carrots, peas, and plums.

Barney was delighted to see a few plump pigeons from their larder. Pigeon trapping was a favorite badger pastime. They borrowed three wicker baskets from the garden shed. They placed the baskets in the shrubbery. Each basket was placed upside down propped up at one end with a stick. They placed a brick on top of each basket, and then baited the trap with corn stolen from the chicken coop. When the greedy pigeons arrived, the badgers pulled a string attached to the stick. The traps closed on the shocked pigeons. Viola, Breakfast!

Barney chatted with his hosts over breakfast. He was very curious about the two hedgehogs curled up in front of the fire. Brian explained that Liam and Larry were their pets. They always carried them on their trips. If the badgers were ever chased by a gang of unruly boys, they would drop the hedgehogs as a diversion. Their pursers would immediately lose interest in the chase and take the hedgehogs home. The badgers would follow them discreetly. The hedgehogs would be fed a very rich diet of lettuce and beetroot. After a few days the hedgehogs would become very gassy and at the first opportunity the boys' mother would place the hedgehogs out in the back garden. That night the badgers would retrieve their pets. Everyone was happy. Billy and Brian were safe. Larry and Liam had been spoiled for two days.

After breakfast Barney was allowed to use the guest bedroom, off the living room, for a nap. He had learned over breakfast that a badger sett had several rooms and three entrances. As Barney dozed off to sleep he thought that his new den should have guest rooms. His hosts had said it was far too dangerous to travel around Dublin in daylight. His quest for a new den would have to wait under after dark.

When Barney awoke he returned to the living room and found his hosts studying a tourist map of Dublin. Paddy had found it discarded on the grass outside the cathedral. They all agreed the best location for Barney's new den was St. Stephen's Green, a twenty two acre park in the center of the fashionable south side of the city. The gates were locked from dawn to dusk allowing the animals to roam in peace, keeping the troublesome people outside. The badgers had started building a sett there years ago in the thickly wooded southeast corner of the park. They had abandoned the sett when they realized that they were too plump to slip out through the park railings at night. They reassured that Barney, being much thinner would have no problem.

There were several ponds in the park and plenty of small animals for the foxes to hunt. Barney wanted to set off immediately to inspect the park. The badgers patiently explained that he was in the city now and they would have to wait until three o'clock in the morning, when the city finally fell asleep. They said it wasn't far to the park and that they would accompany him.

They were setting out for the Wicklow Mountains at the same time and they would be passing St. Stephen's Green. At three o'clock in the morning, a strange procession slipped out from the cathedral shrubbery. Two badgers, each carrying a hedgehog and a fox went swiftly down Wenburgh Street onto Bride, Kevin and finally Cuff Streets to the southwest corner of the park.

After a tearful farewell and a promise to slip into the park before the gates closed on mid-summer evening, the badgers set off on their travels south to the suburbs of Ballsbridge and their delicious organic vegetable gardens. Barney slipped quietly through the railings. He immediately realized that his vixen, Molly, would love their new home.

The park was alive with voles, mice rats, and bunnies strolling around the lawns in the moonlight. It was a fox's dream come true. He cautiously crept into the woods and discovered the abandoned sett. He smelt rabbit. Barney gave two loud barks into the entrance and six terrified rabbits shot out the entrance of the burrow, never to return. He spent the next day sweeping out the sett with pine branches. He added fresh grass and rose petals to dispel any lingering aroma of rabbit.

It was time to return to Rathcoffey and collect his family. He then barricaded the front and rear entrances of the sett with twigs and branches. As a parting gift, the badgers had pressed on him their map of Dublin. He paused and studied the map. He quickly realized that if he traveled south, down Leeson Street from the park, he would come to the Grand Canal. If he turned right, he could follow the canal path to Straffan, a town five miles from home. He set off at three o'clock in the morning, anxious to be on his way home.

At dawn he went to ground in the orchard behind the ancient round tower in Clondalkin. He climbed an apple tree and found himself a comfortable nook fifteen feet above the ground and fell sound asleep in the early morning sunshine. That evening he set off along the canal path until he reached the town of Straffan. Then he raced across open country to home.

As he approached at dawn, he was horrified to hear the terrifying sound of a pack of foxhounds in full cry. It was obvious from a distance that the hounds had finally breached the den in the castle. He could see hounds dashing in and out of the dungeon in frenzied excitement. The hounds then started circling the abandoned mansion. The hunters had dismounted and were trying to remove the old bed frames blocking the hall door. Soon the hounds would be down in the basement ripping his family to pieces.

Barney didn't hesitate for a second. He stood up on his hind legs in the open and barked loud and clear. The foxhounds couldn't believe their luck; a fox in open country. They charged across the potato field with the hunt following in full gallop. His ruse had succeeded. He was drawing the hunt away from his family. He raced towards the eight hundred year old ramparts along the side of the field and disappeared into a narrow hole. The hounds went berserk. They frantically

Barney leading the foxhounds away from Rathcoffey

tried to enter the narrow hole. They didn't realize that Barney had entered a maze of tunnels that ran the length of the ramparts. He was safe and able to recover from the chase. He stayed there all day. The dejected hounds and huntsman ddecided to retired back to the kennels around three o'clock in the afternoon. He knew they would return refreshed in the morning for another hunt. It was definitely time to leave.

Barney finally returned to the mansion that evening. Molly was in despair. She thought he was dead. The cubs, however, were so excited to see him that they forgot their terror at the baying of the hounds at the scullery window. No one could think of sleep, so Barney organized a feast. He told them that all the food in the larder had to be eaten that night as they were leaving at three o'clock in the morning forever.

CHAPTER THREE

D-Day

Three o'clock in the morning, it was time to leave their temporary den for the last time. Barney slipped out the scullery window and checked that the coast was clear. All was calm, no hounds lurking in the long grass. He signaled with his right front paw for the rest of his family to join him. They set off briskly, Indian file, and headed straight across the potato field to the ramparts. They clambered up the steep bank to the footpath and headed south.

They traveled swiftly to Clongowes Wood College, a boys' boarding school, past the school farm which once had been home to the famous "Gollymocky Whale".* (Sin Sceal eile), that is another story. Barney then led them away from the ramparts to a semicircular grove of oak trees and they emerged behind the school cricket pavilion. He then led them into an old den under the cricket pavilion. He had discovered the den several months earlier.

The foxes noticed six field mice fast asleep in a straw nest on the floor. The mice were a great breakfast for the foxes. Barney finally had time to tell Molly and his cubs about his adventures in Dublin with the badgers and their new home in St. Stephen's Green.

Now the challenge was how to safely transport the entire family into the city. The Guinness truck wouldn't be able to safely accommodate them all. If they were discovered in route to the city, there was a real risk of being shot. There was a bounty of twenty euro on each dead fox hauled into the police station. The farmers considered the foxes as vermin and a constant danger to their chickens, ducks, geese, and lambs. Barney, of course, completely disagreed. He felt that the foxes provided a great service by dramatically reducing the rat and field mice population, thus protecting the farmers' precious corn and wheat stocks. Barney also felt it was reasonable that the foxes were rewarded for their services to help themselves to the occasional plump, free range, organic chicken. The farmers, however, disagreed.

* "The Gollymocky Whale" by F. John McLaughlin (LuLu Press)

The cubs spent the long afternoon resting in the long grass watching the school boys play cricket. They had to hide, whenever a cricket ball came near them, to escape discovery.

CHAPTER FOUR

The River Liffey

That night, Barney led his family across the fields to the school boathouse on the banks of the River Liffey. The school boys always carelessly left one or two canoes unsecured and threw their broken paddles into a bin for disposal. Barney explained to his excited family that they were going to Dublin by canoe. He told them that the river originated in the Wicklow Mountains and flowed through County Kildare to the city of Dublin. The river current would carry them to Dublin.

Barney had them launch the smallest unsecured canoe into the river. He placed Molly with a broken paddle in the bow. He explained to her that this was a critical position in the canoe. She was the lookout. She had to peer into the distance and notify him immediately of any potential danger. He then carefully lifted his cubs one by one, into the canoe in a row down the center. He was about to uncleat the mooring line and step nimbly into the stern with his broken paddle when his cousin Roger landed spritely on the dock. His den was a little further up the river. He was delighted to see his relatives.

Roger's favorite sport was fishing for salmon. He had taught himself to lie immobile on the riverbank with one front paw in the water. If an unsuspecting salmon swam by, he would first tickle it gently on the stomach, allow it to relax, and then with a brisk flick of his paw, catapult the startled salmon high and dry onto the riverbank.

Barney explained to his cousin that he was moving his family by canoe to Dublin. Roger was intrigued. He had never considered canoeing as a sport even though he loved the river. He gave the travelers a large salmon that he had just caught for the trip. He told Barney to be on the lookout for weirs on the river. "What is a weir?" asked Barney, suspecting it was some kind of wild animal out to catch foxes. Roger answered, "A weir is a dam across the river designed to raise the water level. He had heard that there were two weirs on the river, one at Leixlip, the second close to Dublin at Island Bridge. Roger said, "You will have to portage around the weirs. Barney was beginning to worry about all these new words he had never heard of before to do with the river. Roger explained that portage meant lifting the canoe out of the river and carrying it down the riverbank until they were below the weir and then relaunching the canoe.

It seemed like a lot of unnecessary work to Barney until Roger explained that the drop from the top of the weir to the river below could be several feet. If they went straight over the weir with the river current the canoe could be destroyed and the foxes seriously injured or killed. Barney thought in that case we will definitely portage.

Canoe portage around Leixlip weir

Barney thanked Roger profusely for all his pertinent advice and for the salmon that he stowed away in the stern of the canoe. Barney said, "Please come and visit us in St. Stephen's Green if you ever get up to Dublin." He then pushed the canoe out onto the current in the middle of the river. They were off.

The foxes were silently swept down the river in the moonlight. Suddenly Molly cried out in alarm, "Look out!" Two large white swans erupted out of the water, flapping their broad wings furiously, as they flew overhead. They saw several otters out hunting for fish in the river as the canoe continued gliding gently downstream. Not one cub slept. They were far too excited by the adventure.

An increasing roar was heard downstream as the current started to rapidly increase. It was now totally dark. Barney decided to plunge his paddle into the water on the port side (left side) of the canoe. The canoe shot out of the current towards the riverbank just before the river flowed over the weir, falling four feet below. The foxes scrambled out of the canoe onto the riverbank, hauling the canoe behind them, just in the nick of time.

Captain Barney then took charge of the portage. He had the foxes flip the canoe upside down. All seven foxes scurried underneath and then stood up carrying the canoe on their shoulders. They slowly and carefully descended the riverbank until they were well below the weir. Barney said, "This must be Leixlip."

As dawn was approaching Barney decided it was time to go to ground. They hauled the canoe into the long grass on the riverbank, upturned the canoe, and then camouflaged the canoe with bracken and grass. They all crawled underneath and fell sound asleep.

Several animals came to investigate the canoe and the dormant foxes. However, when the foxes were spotted, they beat a hasty retreat. The river rats and otters all agreed to let sleeping dogs lie.

That night they feasted on Roger's fresh salmon. Barney hoped they would be safely home in their den by the following night. He then had another snooze before embarking on the next part of their adventure.

They were rudely awoken at dusk by the noise of ducks alighting with a great splash on the river. Barney instructed this cub, Red, to sneak out from under the canoe and slowly crawl down the riverbank. Then he was to pounce on the nearest duck. All was quiet while the fox family waited in anticipation. Suddenly, there was pandemonium on the river! The foxes rushed out from under the canoe. They found Red holding on dearly with his teeth clenched on a mallard's wing. The remainder of the frantic ducks flew off in all directions. The foxes threw themselves into the river to save Red who was sinking and to kill the mallard. They stored the duck in the stern and headed off down the river.

Duck hunting on the River Liffey

By two o'clock in the morning they completed their second portage at Island Bridge weir. They were now all professionals at portage. The river current steadily increased as water from the Dodder and the Poddle Rivers joined the Liffey.

CHAPTER FIVE

Swept Away

The canoe with the foxes clutching onto the sides were swept through the city by the strengthening current. Barney had never considered that the lower Liffey was tidal. The river current augmented by the outgoing tide was six knots. There was no opportunity to disembark. The canoe shot out the river estuary into Dublin Bay and was about to be swept out into the Irish Sea, when Barney plunged his paddle into the sea on the port-side of the canoe. He struggled to hold the paddle upright. The canoe swerved to the left, sweeping out of the tidal current. They were now parallel to the shore. He shouted for his crew to paddle for their lives! They plunged forward in the pitch darkness. They were so intent on paddling that they never heard the sounds of waves breaking on the shore. The fox laden canoe was picked up by the waves and thrown onto Dollymount strand. They were catapulted out of the canoe onto the soft sand dunes. No one was injured.

It was dawn. Barney had the exhausted foxes drag the canoe into the sand dunes and then upturn the canoe and cover it with sand. Their noisy arrival had aroused the curiosity of Seamus and Siobhan, foxes whose den was in the sand dunes. They invited the shipwrecked foxes into their den to recover. They

Foxes being swept down the Liffey and out into Dublin Bay

were amazed to see six hundred multicolored golf balls in piles around the living room. Seamus admitted that he had amassed the collection of golf balls. Their den bordered the Royal Dublin Golf Course. Whenever an errant golf ball landed in the rough, he retrieved it before the golfers could find the ball. If there was a heavy sea mist, he would shoot out of the dunes and retrieve a golfer's drive from the middle of the fairway. This resulted in a double bonus. He would have a new ball for his collection and he was able to listen to an infuriated golfer swear in disbelief at the mysterious disappearance of his wonderful drive from the fairway.

Sean and Siobhan provided the travelers with a breakfast of herring, mussels, clams, and seagulls. Barney added their waterlogged duck from the canoe. After a restful deep sleep, he produced his battered damp tourist map of Dublin. The foxes studied the remnants of the map intently. Barney now realized the critical importance of knowing whether the tide was going in or out. Seamus explained that the tide went in and out every five and a half hours. The foxes concluded that if they waited to launch their canoe until eleven o'clock at night, they would be swept back up the Liffey estuary by the strength of the incoming tide.

All went well with the travelers in the canoe until the incoming tide ran into the outgoing river current. The water was in turmoil. The canoe was stopped in the middle of the river. Again Barney had his crew paddle ferociously for the south shore. They landed on the quay below the East Link Bridge. They tied up their canoe to the dock. It had served them well.

Barney consulted his disintegrating map. He was delighted to discover they were in Ringsend, where the familiar Grand Canal met the River Liffey. He realized if they followed the canal to Leeson Street, and then St. Stephen's Green, they would be home.

Finally Barney's family got a break. They traveled silently along the canal tow path, up Leeson Street to the Green. All was quiet. They slipped through the iron railings into the park. The foxes were incredibly excited. Barney led them through the trees to their new den. They removed the branches blocking the entrance. It was pristine; no rabbits had dared to return.

Molly was delighted with the spacious den, with separate rooms for the cubs and a larder. The badgers had left some matches, newspapers, twigs, and three briquettes of turf beside the fireplace. They had created a chimney out of a hallow log and an old rabbit hole. That night they lit their first fire. They were all able to leave the den and safely explore the park until the gates were opened to let the public in at seven o'clock in the morning.

The foxes breakfasted on two plump pigeons basking in the early morning sunshine. They were safe from the Kildare Hunt and their pack of foxhounds. Dogs in the park had to be on a leash. Thus, they were free from inquisitive dogs sniffing around their den. Every night a cub went out to patrol the periphery of their park. Foxes had to protect their territory. At any sign of an intruding fox, the cub would race home and inform Barney. He would then explain to the visiting fox that this was his territory and tell the fox of other parks that were available in the city.

Twice a week Barney took one of his cubs across the Ha'penny pedestrian bridge to the Moore Street fruit and vegetable market. There was always plenty of discarded produce. They had to share their finds with other foxes living in the city. These encounters were always friendly. There was plenty of food for every fox. They chatted among themselves about their favorite restaurants and hotels with the best piles of garbage. Barney had two favorites, the luxurious Shelbourne Hotel on St. Stephen's Green, five minutes from his den, and Bewley's Cafe on Grafton Street. The chefs in both locations always left out a treat for their nocturnal neighbors. They always returned with small sacks slung over their shoulders full of potatoes, carrots, and apples to add to their larder.

Occasionally, Barney took the whole family on a night walk to Trinity College. They slipped in past the sleeping porter at the back gate in Lincoln Place. Their cubs then played tag with other fox cubs between three and five o'clock in the morning on the cricket pitch. One fox family had dug a den in the Provost's garden and always offered a light breakfast before the visiting foxes left just before dawn. Once a week they visited the large gardens in Ballsbridge to the south of the city. They always returned with paws full of potatoes, carrots, and apples to add to their stores in the larder.

Other fox families moved into the neighboring parks, Merrion and Fitzwilliam Squares. They, however, needed to contend with unleashed dogs whose owners' houses bordered the squares.

CHAPTER SIX

The Strange Tale of Sylvester the Domesticated Fox

Occasionally foxes would drop into see Barney in his den in St. Stephen's Green. Beau, another immigrant from County Kildare, now residing on the north side of the city in Belvedere Square, came to visit.

He related to Barney that there was a domesticated fox living in, of all places, Foxrock, an affluent South Dublin suburb. He was taken out on a leash for a walk by his owner twice a day. Barney was horrified. He was shocked at the idea of a fox living as a dog. He thought that it was extremely cruel to walk a fox on a leash. Something had to be done. Foxes should be free to roam and hunt. Barney decided that he had to go to Foxrock to investigate. He convinced Beau to accompany on the adventure. The foxes poured over Barney's battered map of Dublin.

They discovered that Foxrock was six miles south of Dublin. They followed the railway line to Monkstown, and then headed due west to Foxrock. They arrived at two o'clock in the morning. All was quiet. The town was asleep. Barney raised his head and barked loud and clear. It was a signal to any foxes in the area to come to their help. Two of the local foxes, Paul and Beatrice responded to their call. They lived in a den on Leopardstown race course. They knew all about the strange fox and were able to point out his house. They apologized. They couldn't stay.

That night they were part of a pack of foxes sweeping the race track for rabbits. They had to hurry back to keep their position in the line otherwise the rabbits would escape. Before they left, however, they were able to tell Barney and Beau that Sylvester was often to be found in the enclosed garden behind the house at night. Then Paul and Beatrice vanished into the mist.

Barney and Beau stealthily scaled the garden wall behind Sylvester's house. They were astonished at what they saw below in the garden. A fox wearing a bright red waistcoat and white jodhpurs was standing upright on his hind legs, slowly strolling around the garden. The stunned foxes quietly dropped down into the garden and greeted Sylvester. Barney said to him, "We have come to rescue you and bring you back into the wild." Sylvester amazed his rescuers by saying, "But I have no desire to be rescued. I love my life with the Rodger's family." He explained that both his parents had been killed by the savage Wicklow hounds when he was a young cub. He was forced to leave his cold lonely den to forage for food. He was found starving, rummaging for food in the Rodger's garbage. The family took pity on him and brought him into their kitchen and fed him. After a few days he had his own place at the dining room table. They bought him a dog bed and placed it in front of the fire. The family's only complaint was that the entire house soon smelt musky. It smelt of fox. Mr. Rodgers took Sylvester to the wildlife veterinarian in Kildare. The veterinarian gave him several shots, treated him for worms and, under local anesthetic, removed his musk glands around his tail. There was no longer any smell of a fox in the house. The Rodgers then hired a carpenter to build a swing hatch in the back door to allow Sylvester access to the back garden whenever he wanted. He thanked the foxes for coming to rescue him, however, he said he was perfectly content in his new home and had no desire to return to a life full of uncertainty in the wild.

Barney and Beau left quietly deep in thought. Barney comforted Beau by saying that once a fox is domesticated it cannot survive for long in the wild and that Sylvester was very content with his new life.

When Barney and Beau arrived back exhausted in St. Stephen's Green, they found a rowdy delegation of foxes, from the Moore Street Market, dining on Barney's larder. They had come to seek Barney's advice. They told him that three foxes incarcerated in Dublin Zoo wanted to escape. Barney and Beau were very excited to learn of foxes that wanted to be rescued. They decided to set out the following night to investigate, interview the foxes, and to plan a foolproof escape plan.

Barney and Beau watching Sylvester, the domesticated fox

CHAPTER SEVEN

Dublin Zoo

The following night, Barney and Beau, accompanied by Basil, a Phoenix Park fox, with local knowledge of the zoo, set out on a reconnaissance mission. They traveled single file along the north side of the River Liffey to Parkgate Street. Then they slipped through the gates of Phoenix Park. Basil then took the lead. He led them from cover to cover until all three of them had slipped through the wrought iron railings into the zoo.

They quietly passed sleeping elephants, zebras, penguins, and giraffes. They rounded a corner and suddenly three foxes appeared out of the gloom. They were distraught. They wanted to be released from their cage immediately. Barney told them if they wanted to be rescued they would have to be quiet. Barney, Beau, and Basil explained that they were the rescue committee. They asked the imprisoned foxes to introduce themselves.

The largest fox stepped forward and said, "I am Ronan the red fox from Ben Corr, in Connemara. I was a nuisance to the famous hunt the Galway Blazers. I used to play tricks on their hounds. Frequently, I ran with the pack in hot pursuit of myself. I used to flaunt myself on top of a hillside, when the hounds flew after me in full cry, I used to dodge behind a stonewall and remain perfectly still until the pack shot by. Then I would join them in the frenzied chase. It was great sport. Suddenly, the huntsman would spot me a midst the pack and blow their horn frantically to call back the hounds. When this occurred I would disappear into the mist to live another day. In frustration the Galway Blazers hired two professional hunters, Ginger O'Brien and Greg Little from Galway. They had learnt of my weakness, fresh salmon. I was well known for poaching fresh salmon from the fishermen at Ballinahinch. They laid a trap for me, a beautiful juicy salmon on the riverbank. Without thinking, I rushed forward and grabbed the salmon. A net surrounded me. I was dog meat. An intense discussion ensued as to my fate. Ginger O'Brien and Greg Little argued as to whether I should be thrown to the Galway Blazer hounds or sold to the Dublin Zoo. After a lengthy debate, financial reward took precedence and I was placed in a crate and dispatched to the zoo. For the Littles and O'Briens of Galway, cash is supreme.

The other two foxes emerged to tell their tragic tale. They were from County Meath. They had a great den on a riverbank, well within easy reach of three chicken coups. They helped the local farmers by removing the occasional rooster. However, their rebellious teenagers could not be restrained from raiding the chicken coops. Several chickens disappeared. The foxes were blamed.

One Saturday morning at five o'clock in the morning, the farmers descended on their den. They took the precaution of blocking all the emergency exits then systematically started digging up the den with their potato spades. There was no chance of escape. The foxes were extricated, terrified from their den, and thrown into a sack. The entire family thought their end was nigh. They didn't have a chance to hide the evidence of their guilt. Discarded chicken bones were scattered on the floor of their den. Brian the fox, his vixen, Penny, and their three cubs, Val, Paul, and Ian, were sold to the Dublin Zoo. The entire family were thrown into the mail van of the Dublin express train. They arrived hungry, battered, bruised and traumatized in the zoo and placed in a cage.

Brian and his family hated being on public display from eight o'clock in the morning to six o'clock in the evening. They were not allowed to hide at the back of their cage. Brian said that his family desperately wanted to escape, however, none of them wanted to return to Meath to be hunted by hounds or ignominiously dug up like potatoes out of the ground. They wanted a permanent home away from any persecution.

Barney told the three foxes that help was on its way. The rescue committee would be back in five days time with a plan to suit them all. Barney, Beau and Basil disappeared into the mist, deep in thought. They retired to Basil's den to work out a rescue plan. They all felt that Ronan, the red fox from Connemara, would be a relatively easy rescue. He would be able to hide in Basil's den in the park for a few days. Then when the hue and cry had subsided he would be able to follow the Royal Canal home to Connemara. There was plenty of cover along the canal banks. He would be home safe in his den on Ben Corr, overlooking the wild Atlantic Ocean, within a few days of his escape. They all agreed that the other problem was how to find Brian and his family a place to live free from persecution. Barney thought he had a solution, however, he needed to return to his den in St. Stephen's Green and consult the remnants of his map of Dublin. Beau trotted along beside him. Beau was enjoying his adventure and was in no hurry to return to his den in Belevedere Square where his vixen, Jo, had a long list of chores waiting for him upon his return.

Barney proposed meeting by the graves of the unknown soldiers in the grounds behind Dr. Steeven's Hospital at midnight in two days time. He decided that he needed at least one good night's sleep.

CHAPTER EIGHT

Dr. Steeven s Hospital

All was quiet when the three foxes met on the lawns beside the graves of two soldiers, one English, one Irish. Both of whom had died in the fight for Irish Independence and had been laid to rest together. Basil had built himself a comfortable den in the old vegetable garden of the hospital. If they were disturbed, they could always make a hasty retreat to the safety of his den. Barney opened the meeting by stating that they were going to have to find a locksmith fox to open the old lock on the zoo cage door. Basil said he knew of the ideal fox. His name was Walter. He had developed a talent for picking locks. He had refined his talent by hours of practice. Instead of hunting for food, he window shopped whenever he saw a delicacy in a shop window he went to the side door, picked the lock, and helped himself. Sometimes it was Virginia ham, sometimes pork sausages. He took care to remove any clues of his visit and always carefully re-locked the door. Beau stated that they would have to replace the liberated foxes with decoys to allow their escape to remain undiscovered as long as possible.

Barney was exasperated by this set back to his carefully laid escape plan. Both Barney and Basil asked where on earth could they find decoy foxes? Beau replied, "The Dead Zoo of course." There is even a forgotten baby carriage by the doorman's office for transport. Barney asked exasperated, "What on earth is the Dead Zoo?" Beau explained that he had discovered it one night on one of his excursions from home. He said it was a museum of dead stuffed animals. A hundred years earlier stuffing dead animals and putting them on display was a popular pastime. He said that on the ground floor there was an entire display of foxes and cubs. The museum had been closed for years. No one would miss a few dead foxes. Barney and Basil stared at Beau in amazement. They hadn't realized how resourceful their friend was.

There were only two things left to do. Basil had to recruit Walter, the locksmith, to join their intrepid team. They decided to meet on Sunday night at two o'clock in the morning at the main door of the Dead Zoo on Merrion Street. Beau would spend the next two nights pouring over his map of Dublin searching for a safe secure home for the refugees from Meath. On the second night he found it, Ireland's Eye, an island just off the coast of Houth. It was ideal. It was completely deserted. Only the occasional sailor visited for a picnic in the summer. The offshore island should be teeming with gannets and nests brimming with eggs. Ample food for hungry foxes.

CHAPTER NINE

The Dead Zoo

Basil introduced his friend, Walter, from Kenilworth Square in Ranelagh. Walter made short work of opening the door to the museum. No alarms sounded. They quietly entered the eerie zoo. There were incredibly life like animals, bears, pandas, elephants, giraffes, three floors of animals, staring out at the intruding foxes. Barney mobilized his troops. Beau retrieved the large pram and they carefully loaded three foxes and three cubs from the rural animals exhibit. They would not be missed. No one had visited the gallery for years.

Barney deftly produced a coil of rope. It had three loops tied in it. He explained to the foxes this was going to be their harness. He would be surprisingly enough, lead dog, followed by Beau and Walter. Basil had to tie the bitter end of the line to the front of the pram, and then his role was to steer the pram. They shot out the door, stopping abruptly to let Walter lock the museum door and then through the dormant city. No one was around to see this strange apparition flying past St. Stephen's Green, up Grafton Street to the River Liffey, then along the quays to Parkgate Street into the Phoenix Park. Once safely inside they rested for twenty minutes. Then the baby carriage with its strange cargo of dead foxes was cautiously towed through the side entrance to the zoo. All was quiet. It was five o'clock in the morning, the hour before dawn, the hour of the wolf. No animal stirred.

When they arrived at the foxes' cage, they too, were sound asleep, exhausted by the excitement of escaping. Walter quickly dispatched of the lock. The decoy foxes were carefully carried into the cage. They were placed at the back of the exhibit. From a distance they all looked bored and asleep. They dropped off the pram at the lost and found office. All the foxes silently left the zoo single file.

At Parkgate Street the foxes split up. Basil invited Ronan to stay with him in his den until the hue and cry over the escape had subsided. Barney invited the Meath foxes to stay with him until they could be safely guided to their new island home. Beau finally had to go home to his den and his list of chores.

Pram with stuffed foxes from museum pulled on harness to Phoenix Park

CHAPTER TEN

Swimming Lessons

One night, coming home from hunting, Barney stumbled upon a fight. An otter had a large brown trout in his mouth that he had just caught in the Royal Canal. He was surrounded by six ferocious river rats. They wanted the fish. It was about to get very ugly as the rats moved in for the kill. Barney looking down on the scene raised his head and barked. The rats, recognizing the bark of a fox, vanished. The greatly relieved otter introduced himself to Barney. His name was Niall. He told Barney that if he ever needed his help, he was available. He lived in the canal bank beside the Leeson Bridge.

Well, Barney realized the time to call in his debt had arrived. He realized that he needed a professional swimming coach to teach the Meath foxes to swim. Brian and Jo, sixty miles from the sea, never felt the need to learn to swim. As a result they never could teach their cubs to swim. Times had changed dramatically. In order to be able to swim to their new island home, the whole family needed to learn to swim. Barney realized that professional help was needed. Once the call went out, Niall was there to help. He taught the entire family to swim doggy paddle. In order to humor his students, he called it fox paddle. He had them paddle from one end of the St. Stephen's Green pond to the other, backwards and forwards for hours on end. The mallard retreated on shore in a huff. They wanted to sleep. Niall kept the Mealth fox family swimming from dusk to dawn, seven days a week. After two weeks coaching they graduated from Niall's Swimming School. They were ready for the next part of their journey.

CHAPTER ELEVEN

Claremont Beach

Beau and Barney shepherded the Meath foxes across the River Liffey, out to Clontarf, then along the causeway to Dollymount Strand. Barney's friends, Seamus and Siobhan, alerted by Niall the otter, were waiting to greet the travelers with a scrumptious feast.

At dawn they retired to Seamus's den. Since Barney's previous visit, Seamus had extended his den to include a bowling alley for golf balls. The three fox cubs, Val, Paul, and Ian, played several games of bowling until they collapsed in a heap from exhaustion. The adult foxes poured over the fragile remains of Barney's map. The route was straight forward. They would set off at midnight, travel the length of Dollymount Strand, then swim across to Sutton Cross. They would then follow the Howth Road two miles until they saw the signs for Claremount Beach. Apart from terrifying a few alley cats, the trip went like clockwork. They found the beach deserted at two o'clock in the morning. The cubs were dispatched to search for short pieces of flat driftwood. The sea was flat calm. They all could clearly see the sharp silhouette of Ireland's Eye a mile to the north. There was no time for hesitation after several hugs the intrepid Meath foxes swam out to their new home. The cubs floating on driftwood rafts while their parents nudged them gently over the calm water.

Barney and Beau watched until the foxes were out of sight, then briskly retraced their steps to home. They were surprised by a harbor seal as they swam across Sutton Sound to Dollymount Strand. Everyone was shocked, the seal and the foxes. They took off in opposite directions. Barney and Beau racing each other to the shore. They dropped in to see Seamus and Siobhan to inform them that Brian and his family were safely on Ireland's Eye.

Meanwhile, Brian's family were busy exploring Ireland's eye. After a feast of gannets' eggs they searched for a den. Brian chose a cave halfway up the hillside with a commanding view of both sides of the island. No one could land without being spotted from their new den. They swept the dust out of the cave and laid fresh heather on the floor. They quenched their thirst at a spring beside their cave, then they all fell into a deep sleep, content that they were safe from foxes and huntsman.

Meath foxes swim to their new home

CHAPTER TWELVE

Midsummer s Eve

Calm had returned to St. Stephen's Green. Barney enjoyed reading the Irish Times every evening when the park was closed. The cubs would always find an abandoned copy to bring back to Barney. They all followed with intense excitement the mystery of the missing foxes from the zoo. The editor had concluded that it was most likely a student prank. No one commented on the abandoned pram. The decoy foxes were quietly returned to the Dead Zoo. Locks at the zoo were changed and security with video cameras were installed at considerable expense at the Dead Zoo.

Several weeks later, a strange tale of a fox balanced on a dismounted horse hunting with the Galway Blazers was reported by the Irish Times. Barney knew that Ronan had made it home and was up to his old tricks.

Barney and his family had planned a midnight picnic on the lawn in St. Stephen's Green. They were pleasantly surprised by the arrival of their badger friends, Brian and Paddy, slipping inside the park gates just before they closed. The cubs were delighted to discover the hedgehogs had also arrived. As they were relaxing on their backs, after a scrumptious feast, a thought occurred to Barney. It would be extremely useful if foxes could share the cover of hedges when they were out hunting. He approached his guests, the hedgehogs, and asked them whether they would share the hedge. They both replied, "No."

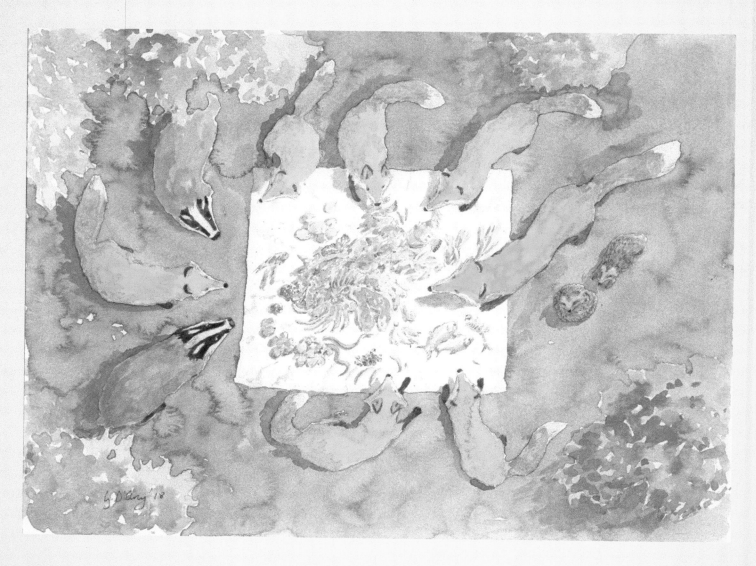

Picnic on the lawn in St. Stephen's Green

Barney departs his home and heads for the city

Lightning Source UK Ltd.
Milton Keynes UK
UKHW021657130920
369623UK00004B/105